Euphony

Micro Prose Poems

Michael C. Keith

BAMBOO
DART
PRESS

LOS ANGELES † NEW YORK † LONDON † MELBOURNE

Into the paradise of euphony, the good writer must introduce Hell. Broken paradises are the only kind worth reading.

—Mark Doty

Euphony: Micro Prose Poems by Michael C. Keith

978-1-947240-91-9 Paperback

978-1-947240-92-6 eBook

Copyright © 2024 Michael C. Keith. All rights reserved.

Artwork: *Appetite for Deconstruction* by Lorette C. Luzajic, 2017

Layout and design by Mark Givens

For information:

Bamboo Dart Press

chapbooks@bamboodartpress.com

Bamboo Dart Press 043

www.pelekinesis.com

www.bamboodartpress.com

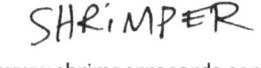
www.shrimperrecords.com

For the Bagel Bards and O'Haras

CONTENTS

MODIFIED

In her fifth-grade grammar class Madeline was daydreaming when her teacher explained the meaning of dangling participles. This gap in her knowledge had no small impact on her adult life.

LISTENING TO MARS

The Mars rover was hit by a dust devil during which NASA scientists captured a scrap of audio. What it revealed shocked them. They would not convey what they heard to the general public for fear of dire consequences. Their good intentions were for naught when an amateur astronomer in New Zealand hacked into their data bank and came across the Martian message. *The Southland Times* was thrilled to have the information it provided and prepared for a special edition of the newspaper . . . which never made it to press.

Days Without Meat

It wasn't a meal to 13-year-old Ernie Ferris without beef or pork. It was the way he and most kids were raised in the 1950s. The only time he had lunch without one or the other was when his mother made him peanut butter and jelly for school. That was acceptable to him. Some kids had tuna salad sandwiches on Fridays because they were Catholic, and that was not acceptable to him, since he hated fish. He was very thankful his family was not religious and knew how to feed their children.

EUPHONY

Serious poets like to pronounce the word poem as po-*em*. I have a hard time saying it that way so say it like an "m" added to the end of Edgar Allen Poe's name. He wouldn't be called Edgar Allen Po-*em*.

Settling for What is Yours

One of my incisors distracts from my looks. I believe if it's removed I will be considered handsome. The problem I have with its extraction and replacement is it will no longer be mine. That is, it will not be natural to me. It will be a foreign object in my mouth. The more I think about it the more I believe it would not be a good thing. Therefore, I have decided to live with being almost handsome.

THE WIZARD OF TRASH

He had a way with words. He could shape them in a manner that would excite racists and the profoundly uneducated. In time, he built a following which supported his bid for the highest office in the nation. To the surprise and shock of those capable of reason and compassion, he won the vote and proceeded to abolish the honor and integrity on which the country was founded. This made his legion of disciples happy as a dead pig in the sunshine.

WHAT KIDS OVERHEAR IN BED OFTEN HAVE A LONG-TERM EFFECT

Sheila's parents loved to play jokes on their nine-year-old daughter. After she was taken Halloween trick or treating by her mom and tucked into bed for the night, her folks stood in the hall outside her room and spoke about the monster they had found under the little girl's bed the previous day. When Sheila grew into adulthood, no one could convince her that parents weren't a nasty, sick bunch of bastards.

Dark Romance

She hid in a culvert and caught her breath while listening for her beau. He was farther off than he'd been, and his threats had turned into pleas that she come back home so they could talk things out. "Bastard," she growled, clutching a rock and running in the direction of his voice.

Unfriended

Bert posted a picture of himself as a young man on Facebook. The reaction of his friends was off-putting, if not depressing. No one could believe it was him. "But you were so handsome with all that hair," posted one person. Another commented, "That can't be you. It doesn't look anything like the guy I know." The response to his long-ago photo prompted him to delete it, but the idea that people saw him as so changed haunted him. It was then he waited in ambush for his friends to post past photos of themselves.

HITCHHIKER MASOCHIST

I stood on the icy highway with my thumb outstretched desperate for a ride soon because I was freezing. When a car finally stopped and told me he was going as far as my destination, I told him no thank you. I was not about to forego the hardships of short rides to where I was headed.

Not So Smart After All

There were no more so-called great innovations. The human race had run out of ideas. All the fields of research ceased to unveil new discoveries. It was the end of advancements or solutions of any kind. After a period of time it was concluded the major human inventions up to the moment of what came to be called the Big Cessation had been over-rated anyway.

In Search of a Safer World

They finally found a planet with no water and were elated and relieved. It was there they would relocate their species of non-swimmers.

INSPIRED LOYALTY

When I was 11, I jumped off the playground seesaw with my little sister at the high end. She hit the ground with a scream and had to be carried home by a neighbor who saw her writhing in pain. When my mother asked what happened she told her she'd fallen, never saying how or why. Even as an older adult that moment remains vivid to me, and I love her better than the rest of my five siblings.

LOOKING UNTIL YOU FIND WHAT YOU WANT

"How many close friends does the average person have?" Marge asked Google. "Between 3 and 5," it replied. This did not sit well with her, so she made another inquiry, asking the search engine how many fair-weather friends the average person has. The answer was more to her liking.

Signals in the Air

In the 1960s, a young Lakota Sioux from the Pine Ridge Reservation attended a meeting of wealthy white entrepreneurs. He carried a proposal aimed at funding the construction of the first Indigenous radio station. When he was asked why it was important to do so, he said to help preserve his tribe's vanishing language and culture. He was asked to provide stronger rationale.

REVELATION

Daryl discovered if he just lip-synched to the hymns he could still be in the church choir. He had to do nothing to make his parents proud of him. It was at that moment he decided it was how he would live his life.

STUCK IN TIME

The clock on the steeple of the Methodist church in the town's square says 4:11. The hands haven't moved in years, at least not since I noticed them five years ago. I ask the manager of the hardware store directly across the street from the house of worship if he knows how long it has been broken. He misunderstands me thinking I'm asking him for the time. "It's 4:11," he says, looking out the window at the church.

GOD IS LOVE?

In recent months, Calvin began experiencing aches in some part of his body until he rose from bed and shook them off. He attributed the "creaks," as he called them, to his hard work and went about his day thinking little of the fleeting pain. Soon the aches began occurring midday, but as they had in the morning they would recede once he stretched and moved about. As evening approached the aches began to recur and he would shuffle about his yard waiting for them to fade. Finally, the day came when the aches would not go away despite his efforts to eliminate them. In his few remaining years, he took comfort in knowing his constant discomfort was what his creator intended.

A MOVING REVIEW OF THOSE IN HIS LIFE

He figured if he sped up he'd be there in less than an hour. Another poke at the accelerator would gain him a few more minutes with his friends. Then he thought about the people he was racing to see, and it occurred to him he'd be better off slowing down.

LATENT EXPOSURE

Something he did decades ago suddenly appeared on his screen. He was totally confounded because he was certain there was no camera in the room where the incident occurred. In fact, there were no computers back then either, he told himself. "How was it possible?" he mumbled, tapping away at the keyboard hoping to delete the image while also being drawn to it. *What if anyone else sees this? What will they think of me?* he fretted. Finally, the image disappeared, and he was left wondering if his sly techy sister had somehow managed to record him trying on her panties.

MAYBE NOT

I like how my new friend thinks. She agrees with everything I say. Her opinions reflect mine on everything from politics to sports. Tomorrow I'll ask her about sex. Bet we're on the same page when it comes to Pop Rocks.

HEEDING THE SIREN CALL

It was the honeyed cantillations from afar that drew the attention of the son of Laertes and Anticleia, taking him off his intended course. Again, the poet sovereign had manipulated his hero protagonist for the sake of classic literature.

Premature Priorities

The Socotra Dragon Blood Tree was all that remained on Tad's bucket list. He had no idea how it got there, but since it was there, he felt obliged to see it. However, getting to where it grew on Yemeni island in the Arabian Sea was not possible because his bank account had been emptied out in pursuit of the other items on his long list. He calculated it would take four more years working at Starbucks to accumulate the necessary funds to make the pilgrimage and he shuddered at the prospect of being 23 years old by then.

CONVERSION

Civil rights activist Zukuma Honn was abducted by a white supremacist group, duct taped to a La-Z-Boy recliner, and forced to watch *The Lawrence Welk Show* non-stop for 11 days straight. When he was released he sent a fan letter to Myron Floren.

A Parent's Experience Deepens Insight

It was snowing at the entrance of our driveway, and it was July. On either side of the swirling white squall, the sun blazed hard. We kids were completely confounded by it and figured it might be the reason people had stopped visiting us. "Of course, it is," said our mom. "Who wants to deal with winter weather in the summertime?" We knew she made sense, since she claimed she'd seen this thing happen before.

An Interview Question Asked of the New Pulitzer Prize Winner

What if people stopped liking you personally for no reason you could understand. Would you not worry about it because it gives you a plot for your next novel?

Unanticipated Attacks

Pale Brits with their bowler hats and umbrellas are taking over trailer parks across America. They're drawn to Airstreams and Winnebagos and lay claim to them, ousting their owners. The Casitas and Scamps so long ignored, even disparaged, are now highly desirable and in short supply.

SOMETIMES MORE THOUGHT NEEDS TO ENTER DECISIONS

Being morbidly over-weight has plagued Bernie throughout his life. He can no longer deal with the problem and has been told that removing certain of his body parts will address it. The bigger the organ or appendage extracted the more the weight loss, adds the surgeon.

EXCEPTIONAL SERVICE

The married couple were waiting for repairs to their dishwasher from a phantom company. The husband called it that because they never saw the repairman. The service promised he'd be at their house between eight and five. He never showed up but the company claimed he'd been there and made the repairs. When the husband protested, the company asked if he could prove the repairman had *not* been there. "Yes, I can," said he, reiterating that the dishwasher *still* did not work. "Oh," said the company, "Do you want us to send the repairman back?"

Milk on the Sill

There was no place to keep it cool. No icebox in our place because we didn't have the extra three dollars a week for a light housekeeping room that had one. Already it was beginning to smell a little off from the heat, but we figured it would keep longer if it were outside. Problem was the sun hit our side of the house all day long. Dad said that's the way luck worked for poor people like us.

REASONS ACCUMULATE

While he loved his wife, he could not stop thinking about other women. Women who were nicer, younger, slimmer, smarter, funnier, wealthier, faithful . . . He wondered why he and his spouse had drifted apart.

This Is the Way the Author Began His Dark Tale

"Phillipa had never seen a child at the house with the toys strewn about the lawn. For years she'd passed the rundown raised ranch and had only occasionally seen an adult emerge. Then, on a blustery winter morning on her way to the market, she saw three life-sized rag dolls scattered amongst the neglected playthings. On her return home an hour later, they were gone, mysteriously reappearing on the front steps of her house. She quickly posted them on eBay. Two days later her next-door neighbor purchased them and placed them in an upright position facing Phillipa's living room window."

WHY THEY FIGHT

It excited the young Brits to sign up for the war. It was where they saw their glory and its dividends. None expected not to return home. None imagined their ladies in waiting mourning them and marrying someone else.

At a Loss for Words

We sit together silently in our parlor. In the other rooms of our house we do speak occasionally. We are aware in the parlor we have nothing to say to each other. It seems for this reason we spend more and more time in there. We reveal this to our marriage counselor, who asks us why we think this happens.

Going Nowhere Fast

It seemed to her his worst temper tantrums occurred while he was driving. She also observed he was very sweet and calm when the car was not moving. It was difficult to convince him to remain in the driveway without going anywhere, but the effort was well worth it to her.

RSVPlease

My family isn't large, but I have gatherings just the same. It's no bother cooking for two. The challenge is getting everyone to come.

1957: South of the Mason Dixon Line

I'm told by the burly bus driver to get my white butt out of the colored section. I ask why, and he looks at me threateningly and says to get up front where I belong. The black passengers look at me with ambivalence while others just look away.

About the Author

Michael C. Keith is professor emeritus at Boston College and the author of over 25 story collections—his latest titles include *Quiet Geography* from Červená Barva Press, *The Late Epiphany of a Low-Key Oracle* from Scantic Books, *Bodies in Recline* from Pelekinesis, and *All the Noise in the Room* from MadHat Press. He has been nominated for an IPPY, a Pushcart Prize, a PEN/Faulkner Award, and was a finalist for the International Book Award in the "Fiction Visionary" category.

Prior to entering the realm of fiction, Keith wrote several groundbreaking books in the field of radio studies, among them the most widely adopted text of the audio medium (*The Radio Station*) and several monographs on the role of radio in culture and society, including a title chosen by President Clinton to appear on his official summer reading list (*Waves of Rancor*, coauthored with Robert Hilliard). For his work in this area he was awarded the Lifetime Achievement Award in Scholarship by the Broadcast Education Association, the International Radio Television Society's Stanton Fellow Award, and the University of Rhode Island's Achievement Award in the Humanities.

His work has been translated into several languages.

BAMBOO
DART
PRESS

112 N. Harvard Ave. #65
Claremont, CA 91711

chapbooks@bamboodartpress.com

www.bamboodartpress.com